Don't forget
to write

A Red Fox Book

Published by Random House Children's Books
20 Vauxhall Bridge Road, London SW1V 2SA

A division of The Random House Group Ltd
London Melbourne Sydney Auckland
Johannesburg and agencies throughout the world

Copyright © Martina Selway 1991

1 3 5 7 9 10 8 6 4 2

First published in Great Britain by Hutchinson Children's Books 1991
Red Fox edition 1993
This edition 2000

Printed in Singapore by Tien Wah Press (PTE) Ltd

THE RANDOM HOUSE GROUP Ltd Reg. No. 954009
www.randomhouse.co.uk

Don't forget to write

Martina Selway

Red Fox

For Rosemary Davidson

'I don't want to stay with Grandad and Aunty Mabel. I don't like smelly farms. I won't have anyone to play with, I want to stay at home!'

'Come on Rosie, Grandad and Aunty Mabel haven't seen you for ages. You'll love all the animals and you'll find lots to do. Now don't forget to wash properly, don't forget to brush your hair, don't forget to clean your teeth and…don't forget to write!'

Griggs Farm,
Arklegarthdale,
Yorkshire.

Dear Mum,
    I didn't want you to leave me at Grandad's. When you went I cried and cried.
    Grandad said, "Come on Old Ginger Nut, dry those tears and let's see if Aunty Mabel has got our tea ready."
    I don't like being called "Old Ginger Nut."
    I want to come home.

Bess and Rags made such a fuss and
licked me all over. Aunty Mabel
told me not to cuddle the dogs
as they had fleas.
Grandad said, "Don't be so daft, a few
fleas never hurt anybody."
I don't want to get fleas
I want to come home.

Aunty Mabel made some toast on the fire and I had one of her special rock cakes. It was very hard. Grandad said, "Mind you don't drop it on the floor, it'll crack the tiles." My wobbly tooth came out.

I want to come home.

When it was time for bed, Aunty Mabel wrapped up my tooth and put it under my pillow for the tooth fairies.

Grandad said, "We haven't had tooth fairies here for years. I hope they find the way."

How will they know I'm staying at Grandad's?

I wish I was at home.

The fairies came! They left me some money, but there are no shops here for me to buy anything.

Grandad said, "We're going to market on Tuesday, it'll have to burn a hole in your pocket 'til then."
I could have gone to the corner shop on my roller skates,
if I were at home.

I helped Aunty Mabel to collect
eggs, she told me to look in all
the dark and cosy places, as hens
laid their eggs all over the farm.
I found a rat's nest in the hay barn.
Grandad said, "Bloomin' pests,
they're a bloomin' nuisance."
I'd like a pet rat,
when I get home.

After tea I went exploring in Grandad's
big cupboards. There was so much to
look at, I stayed up really late.
I told Grandad that I was searching
for buried treasure.
Grandad said, " You're just like your Mum,
Old Ginger Nut, daft as a brush."
I found some funny old photos of you,
I can bring them with me,
when I come home.

We had to get up very early to go
to market. I bought some sweets
and Aunty Mabel bought me a hat
like Grandad's. Then we went to
the cattle market to sell some sheep.
The auctioneer spoke so fast it
sounded like gobbledegook!
Grandad said, "Happen we'll make a
farmer of you yet, Old Ginger Nut."
Next week he's bringing a calf to sell.
It's a pity I'll be at home.

Aunty Mabel made us a picnic today because we had a long climb up the hill to fetch the sheep. It was very hot. All we could hear were sheep munching grass and bees buzzing. Grandad said, "It's going to be a lot quieter next week without you buzzing around!"
I can't believe there are only two days left, before I have to come home.

Grandad said, "It's time we posted that letter. I thought you were writing a book it's taken you so long!"
PLEASE let me stay a little longer with Grandad.
I don't want to come home y<u>et</u>.
Lots of love from
Old Ginger Nut. X

Mrs. A. Lee,
26A Tower Flats,
Molesey,
Surrey.

Some bestselling Red Fox picture books

THE BIG ALFIE AND ANNIE ROSE STORYBOOK
by Shirley Hughes
OLD BEAR
by Jane Hissey
OI! GET OFF OUR TRAIN
by John Burningham
I WANT A CAT
by Tony Ross
NOT NOW, BERNARD
by David McKee
ALL JOIN IN
by Quentin Blake
THE SAND HORSE
by Michael Foreman and Ann Turnbull
BAD BORIS GOES TO SCHOOL
by Susie Jenkin-Pearce
BILBO'S LAST SONG
by J.R.R. Tolkien
WILLY AND HUGH
by Anthony Browne
THE WINTER HEDGEHOG
by Ann and Reg Cartwright
A DARK, DARK TALE
by Ruth Brown
HARRY, THE DIRTY DOG
by Gene Zion and Margaret Bloy Graham
DR XARGLE'S BOOK OF EARTHLETS
by Jeanne Willis and Tony Ross
JAKE
by Deborah King